chameleon (kă-**mee**-li-ŏn) *n*. A small lizard that can change color according to its surroundings. —*Oxford American Dictionary*

Ricky, Rocky, and Ringo's
COLORFUL
DAY

by MAURI KUNNAS

CROWN PUBLISHERS, INC.   NEW YORK

One sunny day, Mrs. Sheep rushed out of her house and screamed, "Help, boys! My colorful chameleon Carl is loose!"

"Don't worry, Mrs. Sheep. We'll catch him!" said Ricky, Rocky, and Ringo. "What color is he?"

m **WHITE**!!" cried Carl.
Try to find me!!"

Hey, boys!" said Marvin the Mountain Lion. "What's the hurry?"

"Mrs. Sheep's white chameleon is loose," Ricky answered, "and we're going to catch him."

"There's no white chameleon here." Carl laughed. "Now I'm **YELLOW**!!"

"Mrs. Sheep's yellow chameleon ran this way. Have you seen him?" asked Ricky.

"I'm here, but now I'm

ORANGE," cried Carl.

"Hello, Mr. Bear. Sorry to bother you. I'm just looking for an orange chameleon," said Rocky. "But I see he's not in your basket."

"Ricky, Rocky, and Ringo!!
This time I'm all **BROWN**!"
Carl giggled.

"Help, police! Did you see a brown chameleon come by here?" shouted the three pals.

"What? Speak louder! Can't you see that our blues band is practicing?" shouted the police officer.

"Excuse me," Ringo said to Paul Parrot.
"Did you happen to see a blue chameleon?"
"No, no, boys! I'm not blue anymore,
   I'm **GREEN**! Try to find me!"

"Did anybody see a green chameleon come in here?" asked Ricky.
"What green chameleon?" asked Carl. "If you mean me, I'm **PINK**!"

"COUGH, COUGH!! Mr. Eddie, have you seen Mrs. Sheep's pink chameleon? COUGH!! COUGH!! He ran this way," said Ricky.

"Wrong again, boys," said Carl. "This time I'm **GRAY** and so are you!"

"Sorry, Mr. Painter, we are chasing a gray chameleon," cried Ricky. "Can't you see I'm **PURPLE**?" Carl laughed.

"We are trying to find a purple chameleon, but it's too much for us." Ricky sighed. "Could you help us?"

"No wonder you can't find him, he's **RED**!"
The fireman laughed. "Here he is!"
"Take me home." Carl yawned.
"I'm tired and very hungry."

Mrs. Sheep thanked the boys, and then they staggered home. Tucked in bed, the shadows were cozy and **BLACK**.

"It sure was a colorful day," said Ricky.

"I wonder what color
Carl chameleon is now?"

"Surprise, surprise!"
WHITE, YELLOW, ORANGE, BROWN, BLUE,
GREEN, PINK, GRAY, PURPLE, RED, BLACK

CROWN, IT'S GREAT TO READ AND LEARN!, and logo are trademarks of Crown
Publishers, Inc.

Manufactured in Japan

Library of Congress Cataloging-in-Publication Data

Kunnas, Mauri. Ricky, Rocky, and Ringo's colorful day. Summary: Ricky, Rocky, and Ringo
help Mrs. Sheep chase a mischievous chameleon as he uses his color-changing ability to
hide from them.
[1. Color–Fiction. 2. Chameleons–Fiction. 3. Animals–Fiction] I. Title.
PZ7.K9492Rh 1986   [E]   85-24250

ISBN 0-517-56125-5
10 9 8 7 6 5 4 3 2 1
First Edition

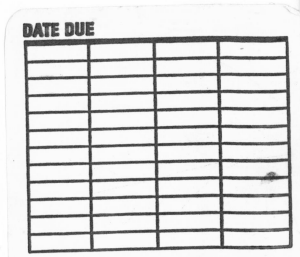

DATE DUE